# SILLY TILLY WITCH

Written by Jennifer Jordan

Illustrated by Ken Morton

Brimax Books · Newmarket · England

Tilly Witch was very cross.
There was a big hole in her roof.
Whenever it rained, water dripped
through all day and all night.
''Drip! Drip! Drip!'' she said.
''I am tired of getting wet.''
So she wore her big, black hat
to keep dry. She wore it in the bath.
She wore it in bed.
She never, ever took it off.

"I must find my Book of Spells," Tilly said one day. "Then I can magic a new, dry roof." She looked under the bed and under the cat. She looked inside her cooking pot and inside her boots. She shook her broomstick and her thick socks. But she could not find her Book of Spells.

Tilly climbed on to the roof
and sat down. "I cannot mend
this big hole," she said.
"I will try to think of some magic."
She sat very still and said
a magic spell.
"Pink jumping frogs,
a blue spotty mouse.
Please magic a roof,
for my little house."
Then she waited for the spell
to work.

Suddenly the roof began to rock
from side to side. Tilly almost
fell off. Then it rose up
into the air and began to fly.
It flew faster and faster.
Tilly held on to the chimney pot.
''I think that was the wrong spell,''
she said. ''Oh, I am a silly witch!''

Sam and Sally Squirrel ran to the top of a very big hill. They saw the roof flying by and waved their arms.

"Our legs are tired," they said.
"We have been running for a long time."
They jumped on to the roof and sat down for a rest.
"Hold on tight!" said Tilly, as they flew through the sky.

Then they saw Mrs Robin.
Her five babies were flying with
her. But they were tired, too.
"Our wings are so small,"
said the baby birds. "We cannot fly
very well."
"Then come for a ride on my roof,"
said Tilly. "We can fly very fast."
There was no more room on the roof
as it flew along.

Katy Kitten was sitting on the top
of the clock tower. She saw the
flying roof go by.
"Help!" she said. "I am stuck!
I cannot get down!"
Tilly picked up the kitten and
went to put her on the roof.
But there was no more room
to sit down. "Katy can sit in my pocket,"
said Tilly. "Now, hold on tight."

Then the big clock began to chime.
BONG! BONG! BONG! BONG!
"It's four o'clock!" said Tilly.
"I must get home soon. My house has no roof."
"But, you're a witch," said Sally Squirrel. "You can magic a new roof."
"I wish I could," said Tilly.
"But I have lost my Book of Spells."

Suddenly the roof began to wobble.
"The magic has gone," said Tilly.
"We are going to fall off!"
The roof crashed into a big, soft
pile of straw. Everyone fell off.
Then the roof rose into the air and
flew out of sight.
"Oh dear," said Tilly. "Now I have
no roof at all. What am I going to do?"

''We can help,'' said Mrs Robin.
All of Tilly's friends took big piles
of straw to Tilly's house. Then the
birds began to weave it.
''This is how we make our nests,''
they said. ''And our nests are warm
and dry.''
They made a warm, dry roof for
Tilly's house.
''Thank you,'' said Tilly.
''How clever.''

Tilly's friends stayed for tea.
It was getting dark when they went
home. Tilly felt very tired so she
got ready for bed. The new roof had
no holes in it.
"I will stay warm and dry all
night," she said. "At last I can
take off my big, black hat."

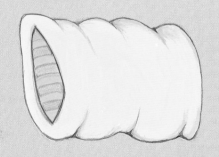

She hung her hat on the door. But as she brushed her hair she began to smile. On top of her head was the lost Book of Spells.
''It was under my hat all the time!'' she said. ''Oh, I am a silly witch.'' Then she put the book under her pillow and fell fast asleep.

# Say these words again.

| | |
|---|---|
| hole | wobble |
| drip | magic |
| mend | rests |
| spell | pocket |
| hill | weave |
| house | clever |
| flying | warm |